280 x 70

280 x 70

Gill James

Chapeltown Books

British Library Cataloguing in Publication Data

A Record of this Publication is available from the British Library

ISBN 978-1-915762-31-3

This edition published 2025 by Chapeltown Books
Manchester, England

Contents

Introduction

This collection is a collection of seventy stories, each 280 words. They were inspired by the first picture seen on my Twitter feed on a given day.

1. Suited

If he just carried on sitting there and grinning it would be all right, wouldn't it? They would think he was fine, wouldn't they? They would assume he'd understood everything, right? He would just purse his lips and nod agreement.

Roberto Alexandro, the current vice-chairman, had a thick accent. He spoke very softly, though, and it always made Thomas want to go to sleep.

He nodded gently and closed his eyes. He wondered whether he looked important enough in his petrol blue suit, with matching polka dot tie and paler shirt. Sure, he looked smart.

He didn't like wearing suits. He always felt cramped. Thank goodness the office had the policy that you could dress casually if you weren't customer-facing. The tie was strangling him. He loosened it a little.

Something changed in the speaker's tone. He sat up and started listening. They would be replacing the chairman the next day. There had been a vote of no confidence.

There was a general murmuring.

"Ladies and gentlemen," said Alexandro, "I know this has come as a shock to you, but if I could have your attention. We shall vote tomorrow. For the next twenty-four hours I will take over the duties of the chair."

"Why wait?" a voice said. "Thomas is here. Won't he do?"

Thomas went hot and then cold. He could hear his heartbeat thudding in his ears. Why would they want him?

There was massive assent. He opened his eyes and found he was not the only one grinning. New chairman, eh? Fancy that.

There was one problem, though. He would now have to wear his suit to the office every day.

He straightened up his tie.

2. Books

Butterflies danced in Maisie's tummy. "A new library just for children," said Papa. "You can read the books there or you can bring them home."

Just for children? And even better, this was something here for her. For once Papa was giving her all of the attention. Normally he was more interested in Robert.

"Is it far?" she asked as she trotted along beside Papa. He walked so fast it was hard to keep up. He was gripping her hand rather tightly as well.

"Not very far at all, sweetheart. You're going to love it."

It looked just like the school that Robert went to, with its red bricks and sash-cord windows.

Robert talked excitedly about books all of the time. "Just you wait until you can read, Maisie. You'll love the adventures." Sometimes he read to her. She loved the stories. Some had lovely pictures as well. The only trouble was he usually picked books about war and fighting. She rather thought she might like something a bit different. She couldn't read, though. Not yet. It seemed to involve staring at the page for a long time. Were the stories supposed to jump off the pages into your head?

"Come on," said Papa. He pushed open the heavy door. It creaked.

Maisie gasped. There were shelves and shelves of books. From the floor to the ceiling. Where had they all come from?

He nudged her towards a table covered in picture books. "Enjoy."

Adventures tumbled out of the pictures. They walked out later with three more books for her to read at home. Reading, she decided, was definitely fun. She must remember not to turn the pages too quickly.

3. Origami

She made long-necked swans, boxes for secrets and delicate flowers. She worked away, folding and creasing. Her tongue poked out and she frowned as she concentrated. The craft paper was gone within three days. She started on the toilet paper and the newspaper.

Auntie Ella drew the line when she started to rip the pages out of books. "You mustn't spoil your books like that. You should have a rest now, anyway. You're going cross-eyed."

But the child just snatched the book back and started screaming. At least the tantrum showed that her vocal chords still worked. They'd not heard her say a word since the accident.

Bob nodded. "It's her way of coping. Susie taught her how to do this. I suppose she thinks it's a connection. Perhaps I can get some more paper from the recycling centre."

"But that will only encourage her to make more and more of these. She needs to get some fresh air. She needs to eat. And she needs to speak."

Auntie Ella bent down and put her arm around the child's shoulders. "We can put them on all of the windowsills and shelves if you like. And what's left over can go in the spare room."

The child stopped for a few seconds, looked up to the left, then shook her head and returned to her folding.

What could they do? She needed help but they didn't know how to give it to her.

Auntie Ella and Bob exchanged a glance. Auntie Ella sighed. Bob frowned.

The little girl stopped folding suddenly. "They're for Mummy."

Later that day the graveyard turned pink and yellow as the origami samples scattered in the breeze.

4. A New Tie

It had been a while since he'd worn a tie. He tended not to, ever, now that he worked from home. But you never forget how to tie a tie. And it would look really smart. His son and daughter still couldn't get theirs right. Or was it some sort of rebellion? He didn't blame them.

He placed it round his neck, made sure that the right side hung down a considerable amount more than left, wound the right side twice over the other one and poked the leftover through the loop. How could that ever be difficult?

It had taken him a long time to find one that exactly matched the Labour rosette. Nothing in his vast collection came anywhere near. He'd found one, though, in the medium-sized branch of a chain store in this medium-sized northern town. They should all cheer, these little northern towns. Salt of the earth people lived there. Real people. Not these Eton-messers.

He was having none of this woman who was causing mayhem. Nor of that silly buffoon who always mussed his hair up before interviews. Nor of that stuck up ponce who sounded like Lord Haw-Haw and had a name like that cat in the picture books written by a Holocaust survivor.

After years and years of blue he'd gone red. A good Lancastrian colour after all. And wasn't his tie a grand example? A true Labour red. He tightened the knot and admired his reflection in the mirror.

Was it time to get the kids out of the grammar school and into the local comprehensive? Quite probably. That woman was enough to put you off grammar school education for life. Certainly.

5. Survivor

You wouldn't have guessed. He is so confident, so self-assured. And he glows healthily. He's pretty fit, too. In both senses of the word. You wouldn't mind a date with him, would you? Of course you wouldn't. I'm lucky. I get to see him every day.

They say that what doesn't kill you makes you stronger. I always thought that was a bit of a cop out or a well-worn cliché. Along with the university of life and the school of hard knocks. He's had them all. But he more than survives. He lives.

But look at what happened to him:
- Abused and beaten by his parents
- No education
- Sold to the slave trade
- Abused by his employers
- Survived an explosion but left blind
- No money available for rehabilitation
- Robbed at gunpoint
- Left homeless and sleeping on the street.

He overcame it all. Now he almost rules the world. You wouldn't want to cross him. Not in a million years. He's a tough one now. He stands no nonsense.

Yet, he's the kindest of men. Rich but doesn't expect people to do his dirty work. His home is open to everyone. He has a guide dog now and supplies many others with them. Always says, "Let me have a look at you." Looking, of course means touching but always in a respectful way. There's a sense as well in which he can look straight through you. He can tell when you're not being genuine.

He gives most of his wealth away. He says, "You take it, honey. You need it more than I do." He says that to everyone.

A true survivor. Big time. Love him! How can you not?

6. Whistleblowing

So, I've done it. There's no going back. The people who need to know have been informed. It's up to them now. Yes, I'm afraid. But I'm brave as well. Actually you can't be brave unless you're afraid. That's what my mother always said and she's right.

I'm standing here with my back to the wall. It's cold and grey. At least I can see everything, though. I can see if they're coming to get me. The law's on my side, isn't it? It will protect me, won't it?

I'm out of a job, of course. They sacked me as soon as I made it clear that they'd been acting illegally, that they'd been telling lies, that they'd been cheating and that they'd tried to deceive people to meet their own greedy ends.

I might end up on the streets. Employers don't like people who've been disloyal to their previous employers.

For the moment, though, I have money in the bank. My parents will help for a short time. They've said so. It won't be forever, naturally. They're not rich. But they've been careful and saved. I don't want to deprive them or my siblings. It wouldn't be fair.

I slip my hands into my jacket pocket. It enfolds me in its luxury. It has a fake fur lining. It's a limited edition designer number. Deep brown and shiny. I wore if for that meeting. It gave me confidence.

I have to tell Amanda now. How will she react? I'd like to think she'll be with me 100%. Or she'll just bundle the children into the car and drive to her mum's.

I'll be left to live on the streets.

7. Gaming

What to choose? He had trained the maiden aunt to send him vouchers for Gaming World. A cheque just get lost in his bank account, went towards paying the bills. He just had to buy another game.

He looked at the display of the latest arrivals. What was it to be? Fighting an ancient monster? Or something spooky – the mystery of a deserted house, perhaps? Who were those hooded figures? The game's title indicated violence. Perhaps not such a good idea. She'd only complain. A quirky red car with a grin on its face might mean his hand-eye coordination would be stretched. That would be no bad thing. That was his excuse for spending so much time on his computer. Then there was that deep space one…

"Come on. Get a move on. The bus is due in fifteen minutes. We want to get a seat."

"Oh, woman. Stop nagging, will you?"

"Well hurry up, then."

He pushed open the door of the shop. Consoles whirred and blinked as gamers concentrated on improving their scores.

Dave grinned at him. "Hi, Sammy. I've got just the thing for you."

"Oh yes?"

Dave reached down under the counter. He handed Sammy a plain DVD case.

"What is it?"

"You'll just have to try it and see."

"The bus...?"

"You won't have to worry about the bus after this." Dave nodded towards an empty console. "It's just a prototype but oh boy, it'll change your life.

Sammy slipped the disc into the DVD drawer. The machine booted up at once and images flickered across the screen.

"Sammy, come on."

No way. He needed a change. He needed to get away from the banshee.

8. Clouds

A clear blue sky. Great wide chimneys belch out what they say is only steam. A threatening black spreads across the sky, obscuring the sun. Oh the irony. The sun gives us life and warmth and light. We create this power to run, heaters, light bulbs and machines that save lives. When everything else goes wrong the sun carries on shining. Except it doesn't now because we have covered it up. We're putting out the sun.

Mary Phillips could not breathe. She could not quite get her oxygen mask to her mouth in time. She died uncomfortably at 4.30 p.m.

Robby McArthur had given up the fags ten years ago but still had a hacking cough. During a coughing fit he lost control of his lorry on the M6 and ploughed into the crash barrier. The lorry jack-knifed. He was killed instantly.

Farmer Peter Robinson's crop failed because there weren't enough sunny days. He couldn't pay his bills. When the bailiffs came, his wife and daughters left in a hurry. He tried to hang himself from the old oak tree in the top field but fortunately – or unfortunately – it was dying and the branch broke.

It carried on going wrong. The squirrels and the birds in Mary's garden realized there was something amiss. The flowers they left for Robby wilted. Peter never saw his family again. It never came right.

No one was aware of the main problem, though: the trees were all dying and soon would no longer be able to turn carbon dioxide into oxygen. And that the sun had had enough of the folly of the human race and had decided to look for a new home.

9. Music Store

She came here every Saturday. It reminded her of her youth. Back in the good old sixties. When she saved all her halfpennies. Every time she'd got enough for a record she'd pop into town to a shop just like this one. She always had enough; she always bought a record.

If she remembered rightly, a single cost six shillings eight pence. "Six and eight," you used to say. That was a real fortune in those days. Well, a pair of smart trousers would cost you 39/11. To be precise, one pound nineteen shillings and eleven pence. A ticket to the gig at the Students Union was £1.50 in today's money.

"What? Big bands like that?" asked her daughter when she explained.

"I suppose that would be about £20 now."

"Even so."

They browsed through the records. She didn't need to listen to them. She'd just read the title and the tune would come up in her head loud and clear.

"Eh, Mum. Do you know this one?" Her daughter had loaded the vinyl and it was now playing.

She took the other set of head-phones. Did she know it? Heck – she'd seen Procol Harem at the Sheffield Students' Union. *Whiter Shade of Pale* had always been one of her favourites.

"1967."

"They did something that good back then?"

"Cheeky!"

"Shall we get it?"

"Why not?" Though God knows how they'd ever mange to listen to it.

"Nice one," said the man at the counter. "That'll be £38.99, thank you."

God, that was a lot of halfpennies. That would have paid for a whole term's worth of Saturday night gigs at the Students' Union or ten nice pairs of trousers.

10. Civil Disobedience

"I don't want to switch the light off yet." Drat it. Mummy was always interfering.

"But you need to be up bright and early tomorrow morning. You like school, don't you?"

Connor shrugs. "It's all right when we have ten minutes silent reading at the beginning of the lesson."

"So what are you reading now?"

Connor nods. "Did you know that dinosaurs were actually covered in feathers and that the birds we have today are related to them?"

"I didn't know that." Mummy takes the book and looks at it. "This is an interesting book. Did you get it from school?"

"Oh Mummy, don't you ever listen? Miss Bramble took us all to the library yesterday and we were allowed to take out one book each. She said we could take it home if we wanted to. Oh, and talk to our mummies and daddies about joining the library. We take the book back when we go to the library again next week. Mummy, can I join the library?"

"Oh, I don't know. We might not have time to take you every week."

Connor growled. "It doesn't cost anything, Mummy. And the books they have are better than the ones at school."

Mummy sighs. "We'll have to see. But for now you must put out your light and go to sleep."

"All right, Mummy."

She leans over and switches off his light. She kisses him lightly on the cheek. "Night-night, sweetheart."

Connor waits until she has gone. He puts his light back on and slides his book from under the covers. He'd better get on with it if he needs to take it back to the library the following week.

11. The Pumpkin

It sat there defiant somehow. Winking and blinking. The biggest pumpkin Jake had ever seen. His grandfather had won prizes for his pumpkins, but he'd never grown anything as big as this.

There were holes that looked like eyes, a nose and a mouth. The top had been cut off too. A candle burned inside. The flesh had been scooped out. Had someone used it for soup?

A group of small witches and wizards by the look of it, and a zombie or two, were making their way along the street. Jake quickly darted behind the bushes.

The smallest witch rang the doorbell. The door opened.

"Trick or treat," called the young monsters.

"My, you're an amazing-looking witch, young lady," said a woman dressed in an ankle-length green dress and what must be a wig of long black hair, streaked grey. Her face looked vaguely green as well. "Now, don't be greedy. Just two chocolates each, now."

Jake's stomach growled. She seemed kind enough. Maybe he could ask her for some of the pumpkin soup.

He waited until the little monsters had made their way further down the street. Then he crept up to the door and rang the doorbell.

The woman in green opened the door but her smile dissolved quickly and was replaced with a look of disbelief. Her eyes closed as she groaned and fell unconscious to the floor.

Darn. Ever since the accident he'd always had this effect on people. No soup for him today then. However, there was a bowl full of chocolate treats on a little table next to the door. He helped himself to two fistfuls. They would have to do for now.

12. Umbrellas

This would do the trick, most certainly. What was there not to like. Books. Coffee. Tea. Cake. How marvellous.

Sally pushed open the glass door and wiped her feet vigorously on the mat. Her spectacles steamed up as soon as she walked into the warmth. She couldn't see a thing. She was aware that her mac and her umbrella were dripping. Her hand found the edge of a chair. She hoped nobody was sitting on it.

"Here, let me put your umbrella in the bucket. Remember it's in the blue bucket. If you ever come again do be aware that you can take one from the yellow bucket if the rain catches you out."

What was this about umbrellas and buckets? She felt her own being taken away from her. She couldn't make out who was speaking but she could see the yellow bucket now. There were dozens of umbrellas there all sporting advertising. What was that all about?

"The advertising pays for the umbrellas. And then everybody can read about our shop as you walk about in the rain."

She could see who was speaking now. It was that sales assistant who was always so enthusiastic.

"Are you here for the event? It's really good value. Tea or coffee, a slice of cake and a copy of the book. Just £5.00."

"Yes, that's right." She proffered her five pound note. Well of course she was.

What a truly fantastic place. She must get the other members of her writing group to come here. Well-known authors and umbrellas as well. What a pity she had her own umbrella with her. She rather fancied doing her bit to promote local businesses.

13. In the Woods

Nicole could hardly see the ground. The cold air hurt as she took each breath. But she needed this: fresh air, relief from the four walls, space to think. She set off slowly.

She knew these paths well. Muscle memory told her how fast she needed to go before she should turn to the right or the left. In the distance she could hear the main road. Civilisation and home were not far away. Except that suddenly it went very quiet.

Had she taken a wrong turning? Had she suddenly forgotten her way? Were those other feet she could hear? Or was it just the echo of her own? She stopped. The other footsteps stopped as well.

She took a deep breath and carried on. The mist was slowly clearing now and the woods were endowed with a soft golden light. The autumn colours were beginning to show. The traffic noise returned All was well. Until she heard the twig snap just behind her.

Her heart thudded into her chest as she turned to look back. There was nothing. Could it have been an animal? Most likely.

She had a stitch in her side. She decided to walk for a while.

Then he jumped out at her. His face was distorted and he looked as if he was in pain. Except that she realised that wasn't it. His flies were open. "Help me," he whispered. He held out a hand towards her as the other carried on its urgent work.

She ran. Out of the woods. Down the road. Into their cul de sac. Up to the house.

Mark flung the door open. "Sweetheart, we need to talk."

She nodded.

14. The Other Children

She'd never managed to see them before. Now they were there, dancing in circles in the bright moonlight. Their clothes were a little old-fashioned. And they were very pale. In fact you could almost see through them.

One of the boys stood still and looked at her.

"Who are you?" she said. "Do you live near here?"

They all started running.

At least she knew where to find them now. They weren't there every night though. But she made her way to the clearing every night there was a moon. The second time she saw them she watched them for twenty minutes before they disappeared.

"Please don't go," she called as they ran back into the woods.

She had to wait another four nights before she saw them for the third time. Were there more of them this time? She hid at the edge of the wood. She could hear their voices but not what they were saying. Sometimes they sang. She wished she could join in.

When she sneezed they ran away.

She didn't see them again for almost a week but on Friday evening she could hear them as she approached the clearing. She didn't hide this time but stepped a little nearer to them. The boy who'd seen her before stared at her while the others crept away.

"I won't hurt you," she said.

He nodded. "Come at the same time tomorrow and we'll tell you who we are."

The next evening they were sitting in a circle when she arrived. The boy gestured that she should sit down. "We are the ghosts of the children who have died in the Benton forest. Welcome to our world."

15. Not in My Name

The orange president grabs the other leader by the collar and shakes him while another powerful figure looks on in despair. This is the way to obtain the Nobel Peace Prize? "There is a ceasefire," he claims while the bombs keep on falling.

My friend rolls her eyes as she sips her coffee. "I'm Jewish through and through," she says. "But this is all wrong. I can't go along with any of it."

An eye for an eye, a tooth for a tooth was the old regime, wasn't it? Now we are taught to turn the other cheek, to walk the extra mile. That of course is New Testament. But whoever Jesus was, he talked a lot of sense. Or is that just because I've been brought up on Christian values?

I remember the explanation of why we need to hold a stock of nuclear weapons. "The others need to know that we have them so that they won't use theirs on us."

So it's fine for us to keep ours but they're not allowed theirs? And the weapons of mass destruction that almost made us outcasts didn't even exist anyway.

"The Holocaust was terrible," says my blond-haired blue-eyed Jewish friend. "But what they're doing now is unforgivable. There are wrongs on both sides."

"Right as well?"

She nods. "That too."

Just stop it, please, all of you. Stop sending young people to fight your silly battles. Stop killing and ruining the lives of ordinary people.

"Have you noticed?" my wise friend continues. "They're all beset with problems. Bad childhoods. Academic failings. Poor self-esteem."

"And they're taking it out on the little people."

"Not in my name."

"Nor in mine."

16. Film Festival Under Threat

They are smiling. Behind them boards name all of their sponsors: a well-known football club, a local letting agent and a popular radio show. They wear their uniform proudly: a golden antenna on a black background.

The audience roars. The applause deafens. It's all over too soon. Something darker follows. The chairman can see the man from the council waiting for him.

"We bring hope and purpose to the young people of the boroughs," says the chairman.

"We're charging everyone the same," says the man from the council. "You have to pay the fees that others pay."

"But we do the rating ourselves."

"How can we be sure you're doing it correctly and you're not harming young people through neglect?" The man from the council keeps his fingers crossed behind his back. Young people will be harmed if they can't pull in more money.

The chairman looks at the figure on the letter the man from the council has given him. "This will close us down," he says. "It can't be done. Hope and purpose will be lost."

Another hovers behind them. He has a familiar face.

"May I look?" asks the super-star. He studies the paper they show him. He taps on his phone. "There," he says. "It will be in your account by tomorrow."

The chairman and the man from the council shake hands. The super-star pats them on the back.

130 films are shown and the two little cinemas are packed each night. They are all genuine enthusiasts not just the film-makers that provide but a small presence at most other film festivals.

There is hope and purpose now for the young people in the two boroughs.

17. Dream Time

She hadn't heard of the writer before but the book was brand new. The word "Christmas" helped. The picture was lovely, too. A street in a small town or village. All covered in snow with a pine tree looking like a natural Christmas Tree.

The heating was on. It was getting dark. She'd picked up Stollen and Lebkuchen from Lidl's on the way home. The hot chocolate was ready. She pulled the little table nearer to the sofa and curled herself into it.

She opened the book with some considerable difficulty. The spine was rather stiff. It was quite hard to keep the page open and eat her cake at the same time. The plastic sleeve the library had provided made the spine even stiffer. She found it hard to get into and had to read the first few pages several times.

Yes, all right. Now she began to get the gist of it. But when was something going to happen? She preferred those stories that plunged right into the action. There was some nice scene-setting here but absolutely no action.

She'd finished her cake and hot chocolate but was still angry. These characters didn't work. They were wooden stereotypes. Besides, people didn't speak that way. Why was the writer telling her all this? Why didn't she show us? She was missing so many opportunities to show us some dramatic scenes.

She slammed the book down in frustration. She could do so much better than this.

She returned her mug and plate to the kitchen. She made her way up to her study. Her computer was already booted up. Right, here she went. She would write her own Christmas story.

18. Flowers on the Table

Nancy frowned. There was something not quite right but she couldn't quite decide what. She was giving Great Aunt Miranda the room with the lovely view over the undulating hills towards the restless sea. She'd remembered that Great Aunt Miranda preferred blankets and a bedspread to a duvet.

She hoped Clive would get on with Great Aunt Miranda. Clive didn't even have ordinary aunts let alone great ones. He had no relations at all. He'd been brought up in a children's home. Quite the opposite from him Great Aunt Miranda liked to go to bed early and get up early.

She picked up one of the books she'd put by her aunt's bed. A harmless romance without any sex in it. She'd checked everything so carefully. Not too much violence in the whodunits either.

Oh dear though, might the criticism be that it was all too tame? It was quite difficult getting the balance right.

At the edge of her mind she could hear her aunt's voice reciting a poem. Something about flowers in a basket and the key of the kingdom.

That was it. She just had enough time to arrange some flowers before her aunt arrived.

Great Aunt Miranda looked round the room frowning. "Those will have to go." She pointed at the flowers. "They'll make me sneeze. Hmm. Same old, same old. You could have got me something a bit raunchier." She put down the book she'd been holding. "Next time, my love, get me one of those nice duvets. Blankets are for old people."

"Okay, Auntie, I hope you sleep well."

"I will if you don't wake me up at your usual stupid o'clock. Night-night, darling."

19. The Woman in Red

She was a tall woman and she held her shoulders back proudly. Her dazzling red dress swirled around her legs as she moved quickly. Who was she? Why was she dressed so strangely? His own Edee would not dare to wear something so daring.

The answer was obvious: this dress empowered her.

He couldn't help but follow. She dashed down streets and crossed broad alleys. They arrived in places they could have got to sooner. He noticed, though, that she stopped every so often and muttered something under her breath. The lights would go out in nearby houses and the people would protest.

He could smell smoke, taste it even. He began to realise that every house at which she stopped had started to burn. Whatever she muttered put the fire out. Was this some sort of magic?

People were piling out of the houses on to the streets now. They began to fight. When she raised her palm, though, they stopped. The fights were erupting so quickly now that she could hardly keep up. He knew that he should serve. He held his bow and arrow ready.

Suddenly she noticed him. She bowed and a thin smile appeared on her mouth.

He took his bugle and blew on it fiercely. The crowd quietened. "Let the lady speak," he shouted.

She stood even taller now. "My friends, these fires are the manifestation of the evil in your hearts. Cleanse your hearts and you will be left in peace."

The town's people bowed their heads and one by one made their way home. The flames and the smoke subsided.

She touched his arm. "Thank you for helping your queen," she said.

20. Seasonal Shop

Offers everywhere, it seemed. That turkey was half price? Who needed that many parsnips anyway? Two for one. Huh! Smoked salmon as a starter? On Christmas day? Cava as an aperitif? What had happened to good old sherry?

Best stick to her list. Rather short actually. They were getting a turkey from the butcher. Their son was bringing the booze and their daughter was supplying the deserts.

She just wanted to get her few bits and bobs and get out of here. Wait, though, shouldn't she get some more wrapping paper? Just in case? Oh, and those mince pies looked gorgeous. Why not get some? It would save the bother of making them.

The list was soon forgotten. The trolley became harder to push. There was the smoked salmon after all. A couple more selection boxes for each of the grandchildren. Baileys on offer. A family board game.

She wondered how she was actually going to manage to lift this lot into the car.

"Spare a few coppers, lady?" That homeless chap who slept in the entrance to the supermarket. He made her shudder. He looked so much like her own dad.

What could she give him? The raw parsnips would be no good. The salmon was too rich. He'd probably like the Baileys but she wanted to offer something more substantial.

"Help me with this lot into the car and I'll pay you." Would he only spend it on booze? Well his choice.

"Ooh, selection boxes," he said as they stashed the bags away. "I loved those when I was a kid."

She thrust one into his hands.

He beamed at her like an excited kid. "Thank you, ma'am."

21. Pre-Christmas Visit

The annual pre-Christmas visit. The house felt cold and damp. There was clutter everywhere.

His father was frail now but terribly independent. He refused to even have a cleaning lady.

"Why don't you move nearer to me, Dad?" said Tobias.

He father shook his head. "I like it here." He pursed his lips and stared into the distance for a few seconds. "Come on, I want to show you something."

His father struggled painfully upstairs. Once on the landing, he pointed to the hatch into the loft. "It's still there you, know. Pull the ladder down and then you'd better go up behind me."

What was still there?

He held his breath as the old man made his way gingerly up the steps. "There," said his father as he arrived in the loft. "It's all boarded you know. You can walk about up here. And here she is."

The old key board. It was a bit dusty but it still looked the same.

His father dusted the keys with his sleeve. "I played her the other day and she sounded as good as ever."

What? His father had been up into the loft on his own. He pulled up the stool and started playing.

Now Tobias remembered. All the ones he used to sing with his parents:

Pack up your Troubles in Your Old Kit Bag, Goodnight Sweetheart, and yes, of course, because it was almost Christmas, *White Christmas.*

"Come on then. What will it be?"

"How about *Jingle Bells?*"

They sang and played for over an hour.

"I could do with a beer," said his father.

"Okay," said Tobias, "you get the beers while I get this thing downstairs."

22. The Trouble with Small Towns

It's really peaceful here. Everything pretty well closes by 6.00 p.m. and you barely notice the rush hour. There are never queues at the supermarket, not even just before Christmas. The air is fresh and you can really breathe. And everyone knows everyone else. Folk look after each other.

So it was a bit of a shock when the Smithins had both of their cars stolen.

"Just be thankful that they didn't hurt you," the local policeman said. The conversation continued that night at the pub, because PC Winkworth happens to be the Smithins' neighbour.

It was outsiders, opportunists. Nobody who lived in the town would contemplate such an act. But what about the Jacksons' cat? That was really nasty. Poisoned, the vet had said. No doubt by someone who knew them and had a grudge. Who would think such a thing could happen? Someone knew exactly when Tibbles would be fed. They'd got into the house and doctored his food. Who would contemplate such a thing?

Then there was Miss Tailor's washing. Slashed to pieces on a Saturday afternoon. Sheets ripped through, dog pooh smeared into her underwear and pig's blood, they established after analysis, thrown over her fancy silk blouses.

When things like this happen in small towns you start suspecting the people you've been mates with for years.

So, I'm leaving. Yes, okay, so then they'll guess it was me. The newcomer. It makes me laugh just how easy it was. How much they all welcomed me and trusted me. But they'll never find me. The pay-out for the cars means I can lie low for decades. You see, everybody tells you all of their secrets here.

23. Recharging Ricky

"So, watcha got for me today, then?"

Ricky clearly hadn't enjoyed his birthday party yesterday. Too many people probably and too much fuss. It wasn't Ricky's style. He looked exhausted. His 100 years were showing. He was slouched in his chair. His mouth was set in a firm line and his eyebrows threatened a frown.

Neil showed him the book.

"Ah. Poems then. I enjoyed her novels."

"I think you'll enjoy these as well."

Ricky sighed. "Alright then."

Tom began reading." We came from the far side of the river / of starlight… thinking about compassion. / A firefly in a great dark garden. / An earthworm naked / on a concrete path." An undefined future is the focus of the third part of the poem, where the speaker reflects on the unfathomable: "I think of the journey / we will take together / in the oarless boat / across the shoreless river."

After twenty minutes Tom paused to look at Ricky. His cousin's eyes were closed. Tom shook his arm. "Eh, fella, are you asleep?"

Ricky shook his head. "No, no. It's easier to get the picture in your head if you close your eyes. Carry on. Carry on. Her poems are even better than her stories."

By the time they announced that lunch was ready Tom had read three quarters of the book.

"Can we finish it after lunch?" asked Ricky. His eyes were shining now. He pulled himself without any effort out of his chair. "And you'll join me?"

"I should think so," said Tom. All those other appointments could wait. And he would make sure he came to read to Ricky at least twice a week.

24. Old Bones

It came to us all. Ashes to ashes, dust to dust etc. Amazing though. You could see where the eyes would have been. This one still had all his teeth. He assumed it was a man's skull, though he couldn't say why. There was a hole where the nose would have been.

He remembered seeing other remains without life. All of those old graves in old churchyards the Republic of Ireland. You could look right into them and see the skeletons. They hadn't used coffins. Then there were those curious underground tunnels in Vienna where the air had preserved flesh as well. Dried out bodies but still bodies. Odd that in some places they'd put all of the skulls together, all of the thigh bones and all of the pelvic bones etc. Why had they done that?

He shuddered as he remembered seeing his mother in her coffin. His father had insisted. "We've got to make sure they've get the right body in there?" Did they have to? Did it really matter?

He touched the skull again. It felt solid but he thought it might be brittle. It was really odd how normally everything else rotted but the bones remained.

"Nice to meet you," he mumbled as he put it back down.

He was inside his head. Who was he, really? Whoever he was inside this body and it suddenly felt decidedly odd to him having a physical body. He shivered. Better get out of here.

The sun was bright outside and he had to screw his eyes up against it. He couldn't shake the feeling, though, that he was really from somewhere else, that he didn't really belong here.

25. The Men in Red

The great door swung open at last and he was allowed in. Their red robes, made of thick woven wool, were finer that he'd ever imagined. The men in the front row were kneeling and had their arms crossed over their chests. They all wore masks. He looked at them all carefully but now he could recognise no individual.

A man wearing a slightly different mask held up his hand up in greeting. "Welcome Jason of Wellington. Are you ready for the interrogation?"

Jason nodded. Would he get the answers right? So much depended on it.

"Where is the best source of gold?" asked a man on his right.

"It comes from the soil. It grows in the fields and in nature."

The man bowed and stepped back.

Now someone came from his left. "What is the order of priority?"

"The universe, the planet, the immediate community, friends and family and last of all self. Though we need also to look after the self so it can make its contribution to the world."

This man also bowed and stepped aside.

"What is the first principle?" asked the man with the strange mask.

"That God is love and love conquers all."

All of men now stood up and cheered. As the cheering subsided the man in the strange mask stepped forward. "Jason of Wellington, you have answered wisely. We welcome you to the Red Order and the Freedom of the Universe."

Seconds later other Red Knights helped him to dress. The clothes felt odd at first but it had been so easy to answer the key questions. Now he would be able to find out what they were really all about.

26. In the Woods

She was lost. She kept going east. The woods were to the west of the town, weren't they? But it was getting dark now.

Then she saw it, the A-frame house. The windows were lit up. Logs were stacked up on the veranda and she could smell wood smoke.

She hurried up the steps and knocked at the door. No reply. She looked up to the upstairs window. Were they asleep? "Can you hear me?" she called.

Still no reply. She pushed the door open. It wasn't locked.

A fire burned brightly in the log-burner. Someone must have lit it. She could smell cooking as well. Garlic. Herbs, maybe meat.

There was note on the table. "Help yourself. I'll be along later."

A few moments later the oven pinged. The food was done.

She waited. It was soon dark outside. She was hungry now. It didn't seem as if anyone was coming to eat the meal.

She found oven gloves, cutlery and a bowl and helped herself to some of the casserole. It was delicious but it made her sleepy.

She made her way up the stairs.

The bedroom was sumptuous. A thick duvet and big plumped up pillows. The ensuite was equipped with soft towels, a fluffy dressing gown and a power shower. After she'd showered and returned to the bedroom she saw the night shirt. Had that been there before?

No matter. She was so sleepy now. She slipped it on and climbed into the bed.

She awoke with a start.

"I knew you'd come." This wasn't Goldilocks or Hansel and Gretel. Trevor. The reason she'd run into the woods in the first place. This was the nightmare.

27. A Space of His Own

It was grey on the outside but the pictures Dylan had seen of the inside were promising. Did he really belong here, though? This was right, wasn't it?

He pushed the door open.

Yes. It was just like the photos he'd seen. Thick carpets in the lounge areas and hardwood floors in the work pods. Gentle muzak. Smartly-dressed receptionists. Purposeful busyness.

"Can I help you?" She didn't look as if she'd take any nonsense.

"I'm here to see Matt Schandler."

As he'd expected. Designer suit. Designer hair style? And expensive aftershave.

"Do you think you'd prefer hot desks for you and your company? Or are fixed ones a better option?"

"Oh we'll hot desk. I expect we'll be in the theatre a lot. How easy will that be to organise?"

Matt grinned. "It should be all right if you book it far enough in advance. Would you like another look?"

He nodded.

Seconds later they were back in the theatre. Yes, it would do very well. The tiered seating was flexible. Stage blocks meant you could set any sort of scene that you wanted. The decor was young and energetic.

"Well, how many slots?"

Dylan's palms were sweating now and he had a lump in his throat. This was going to cost a lot.

"I'd book sooner rather than later," said Matt. "This space is popular."

Oh heck. He'd got the money from the Dragons, hadn't he? They expected him to spend it all wisely didn't they?

"I'd like to book it out completely for the next three months, and fifteen hot desks for the same period."

Matt's eyes grew round. Then he laughed and nodded. "Way to go, man."

28. Sight Restored

They had all told him he was mad.

"Just get some new varifocals," said his father.

"What if it doesn't work and you've spent all that money?" said his wife.

"Dad, you'll look crazy without your specs," his fifteen-year-old son said.

Well he was here now. It was a swanky place, actually. Thick carpets and sofas you sank into. Piping hot coffee and nice biscuits on the go. He was dressed smartly enough but he guessed the other patients' clothes didn't come off the peg.

He didn't have to wait too long. Soon he was in the luxurious treatment room. His chin was held in place with a rest and a band across his forehead, and struts at the side of his face stopped his head moving. The white purple-rimmed light came at him.

"Just creating the flap now," murmured the surgeon. "Good, and now the other eye."

The light came again.

It was painless though puzzling. Would it work ,though? He'd read about possible side effects. Seeing halos. Not being able to drive at night. Fluctuating vision.

"All done. You'll need to use these drops as your eyes will be dry for a while. I'll see you in two days' time and then again in six months. But it's all looking good at the moment."

Later he noticed the brightness of the flowers in his garden. He admired his daughter in her prom dress. He fetched her back later when she and her boyfriend had a massive row. There was no problem with driving in the dark. He didn't even have trouble with the promised dry eyes.

"So worth it," he told his wife. "I can see clearly now."

29. The Girl with the Blue Hair

He'd been dreaming again. Partly pleasant. Partly not. The same as many times before. Familiar, certainly. What did dreams ever mean anyway? Just processing wasn't it? If only he could remember what though.

Think. Then it hit him. The girl with the silky blue hair. Yes, every night now for over a week. But why did he always forget? How could he? She was lovely. Her long hair tumbled over her shoulders and framed her face. It glistened shades of blue and silver but mainly blue. Her face was perfectly shaped. Her eyes were kind.

She never spoke. She just stared at him. It was as if she understood him and he understood here. They didn't need to speak. They were one.

She held something in front of her. A glass bauble, perhaps. A large one. Maybe it was a sort of snow globe. Liquid or air swirled round it and when it gradually settled there was a letter S in a glittery material. Was this some sort of crystal ball? What could it mean?

Well he would have to forget it now. It was time to get the day underway.

"Emergency!" said Sonya, his office buddy. "I need a plus one for the staff awards tonight. Everyone else is taking a partner. "I'll look silly without one. How about it? Please?"

He reluctantly agreed. He hated these corporate events.

"I'll meet you there. I'm having my hair done first."

By seven that evening he was loitering in the reception area of Statten Grange. He hoped she would be on time.

A taxi arrived. Out stepped a glamorous young woman with long blue hair. Sonya. She smiled knowingly at him.

30. Just Two Days

"I'll be blunt. You have just two days' worth of oxygen left. We're truly sorry." The commander's face was grey and he was frowning slightly.

"Thanks for letting me know." This sort of end had always been on the cards. They were prepared. That was why his salary was so high and his pension would carry on at exactly the same rate. At least Susie and the kids would be fine.

"Make yourself really comfortable. Shall we keep in touch?"

Brad shook his head. "No, it would just be a reminder."

"All right. Call us up if you need anything. And we suggest instigating protocol 500 in thirty-six hours."

"Will do."

The vintage champagne had been supplied for when the centre was fully open. Well, that wasn't going to happen now. After three quarters of the bottle he began to feel a little light-headed. Best get something to eat.

Th smoked salmon and caviar was just right.

He watched his favourite old films noir: *The Wolf Man*, *Le Corbeau* and *Arsenic and Old Lace*.

He wrote a long letter to Susie and slightly shorter ones to Beth and Sam.

Thirty-three hours passed really quickly. He looked at the instructions for protocol 500. He would just have to attach the tube to the permacanula. They suggested then lying down and listening to music of his choice. Simple enough really. He had a play list of soothing classics. That would do nicely.

He broke open the sterile packaging and was just about to insert the tube when the communicator buzzed. The commander again. "Hold fire, Jackson. We've rectified the fault and your oxygen supply will be back to normal in two hours."

31. 23 February

She got the flu within three hours of having the flu jab. "No, no," the chemist had said, "you would have had it worse if you hadn't had the jab. Believe me."

But she didn't. She was sure that that jab had caused it all.

The runny nose, the fever and the hacking cough passed. But a cough continued. She felt as if she constantly had fluid in her throat. Sure enough, when she coughed she could taste it.

Worse than that though were the aches and pains all over. First it was her knees. Then her hips. Sometimes her arms would feel too heavy to lift, Then there were the strange shooting pains through her head.

"You should go and see the doctor," her husband said.

"No, they're far too busy. Anyway I don't think they'll believe me."

The truth, though, was that she felt too tired to go. It would be an effort to get into the car, find a parking space and then walk the distance from the car to the surgery. And that was the other thing. She was so tired all the time. She just wanted to stay in bed or curl up on the sofa and watch old episodes of *Poirot* or *Morse*. At least she didn't have to worry about work. She was retired now.

"There's an article in the paper today," her husband said one Sunday. "Seems it does exist. Chronic fatigue syndrome."

He read out the article as she gazed out of the window. The spring had arrived. It might be nice to get out.

"If I make an appointment will you take me to the doctor's next week?" she asked.

32. Yellow Sky

Tom had read about yellow sky and he'd seen it on book covers. He didn't think he'd even seen it in a movie. And here it was now. Was it the effect of the setting sun?

The normally browny-grey stone of the walls on the promenade was scarlet against the yellow background. Were his eyes playing tricks on him? Didn't the sun set over the mountains and not the sea?

He shivered. It was bitterly cold out here. No wonder he was alone.

Should he quit? Couldn't he do an on-line course from the comfort of his own home? Wouldn't that be cheaper as well? Even if it meant he couldn't have Professor Rob Travis as his mentor? A Masters was a Masters, after all.

Maybe he should sleep on it. And he should eat. The cold air was giving him an appetite.

He turned his back to the sea. He heard running footsteps.

"Hey there," a voice called.

He turned and saw another student from the short-story class he'd attended earlier, about the same age as himself, he guessed." How's it going? I'm Ralf. Ralf Anderson, by the way."

Tom took the extended hand and shook it.

"I was an undergrad here," said Ralf, "so I'm used to it. It's a bit bleak isn't it? But it's cosy. We're all eating at the Silver Duck tonight. You should join us."

The Silver Duck was lively. Tom soon spotted some of his other classmates and sitting in the middle of them was Professor Rob Travis. Cosy.

He glanced back at the window. The stones on the promenade had returned to their normal grey and the sky was now dark blue.

33. Our Betty

There she is. Smart old-fashioned hair, set and naturally white. Her glasses make her look intelligent. My friend's mum always said that specs had that effect. You wouldn't mess with her, would you? 1992 she took on that role. I was just starting to be middle-aged then and to take politics seriously.

Of course she'd been our MP since 1973. And she was an MEP for a couple of years. Well, there's one good thing about West Bromwich; everywhere you go afterwards is an improvement. Even Salford? Yeah. Even Salford. At least it's got a cathedral and the Ship Canal. What's West Bromwich got? Well, at least it had our Betty for a while.

Did you know she's against Brexit? She doesn't look like a Remainer, but there you go. "Nobody voted for this mess," she says. "I blame the charlatans who peddled the falsehoods that [Brexit] would be easy. I wouldn't trust them to run my bath, let alone the country." Hear hear! Woman after my own heart. Go, Betty.

She's had some praise from high places. Tony Blair, the Prime Minister when she resigned, paid tribute to her as "something of a national institution". Blair's predecessor, John Major, described her as an "outstanding Speaker".

That cry of "Order! Order!" I've not heard anyone do it better. You need someone strong to keep that lot in check. I wish she'd come back and sort them all out. They're a right shambles now. Piss-ups and brewery fails come to mind.

Do you know she used to be a Tiller girl? Yes, for eight years she was a dancer. Her name makes her sound like a cartoon character don't you think?

34. Dangerous Currency

Everyone knew that they weren't real. You only exchanged them in cyber space. If you could. They did look smart, though and huge. Bigger than the old half-crown. And with such intricate etching.

"Well, what do you think? Will you buy some?"

"How do I know you're really from the bank?"

"Tell you what. Look up the bank's phone number and phone it. Ask for Ray Drummer."

"All right I'll do that."

David felt uneasy. Wasn't there something about them keeping the line open? That you thought you were making a new call but in fact you were still hooked up to the fraudulent caller?.

The bank's number was already in his mobile. So he would use that rather than the land-line. He speed dialled it.

"You're quite right," said the woman at the bank. "We have no one called Ray Drummer working here."

"Can you do anything about it?"

"Not usually. But we just might be able to do something today. Go back to your land-line. Keep Ray Drummer on the phone and keep this line open as well."

It was so easy. He spoke to someone else first and then he was put through to Ray Drummer again.

"So how many would you like? And how will you pay?"

"Can't you just take the money out of my bank account?"

"You'd have to let us have the pin number from the card."

Like heck he would.

"You're doing fine," said the woman from the bank. "Try to keep him on a little longer."

"Well, I'll have to go and look them up."

"What the fuck?"

David smiled to himself as he heard the police sirens in the background.

35. Plastic in the Sea

It was a strange thing. Like nothing they'd seen before, yet it seemed familiar. It had arms or maybe they were tentacles. They waved around anyway in a mad, happy dance. It was bright like the sun.

The little fish gathered round each day to stare. They didn't go too close. It was bigger than them. It might attack. But it might be food. Best wait and see. And still it danced and waved and waved and danced.

It was battered against the rocks and attacked by bigger fish. Bits flaked off. It started to fade. Perhaps it was dying. Small pieces floated through the water, hardly sinking, but certainly moving towards them.

One brave fish swallowed a lump. Then another and another. More fish came. It didn't taste of much bit it filled a hole in some hungry bellies. Fewer and fewer fish came over the next few days. Maybe it just wasn't so interesting any more.

A dark shadow passed across the water. The little fish dived away. They didn't want to be eaten. Wasn't it too shallow for him here, anyway?

Now there was nothing but the big dark mammal and the strange faded orange creature. There was a terrible gnawing in its belly. It didn't feel right. Maybe if he could eat he would feel better. He saw the strange shape and snapped his mouth round it.

It was almost impossible to swallow. It seemed to fight with him but eventually he got it down.

But he felt heavy inside and longed for sleep. He surfaced and dragged himself on to the shore.

"Plastic in his belly, no doubt," said the human who examined the corpse.

36. Dropbox

It was a wonder, a joy to behold, a thing of beauty and other clichés. It was a third back-up, after saving to the computer's own hard disk and the attached memory stick. Now as well she could access her work from any computer anywhere in the world.

She added in all the music files, the sheet music and the MP 3 files. Just as long as he remembered to have headphones but she felt she had to replace the ones that came free with her iPhone.

She uploaded files of free stuff, enticing people on to her newsletter. Maybe she could add a new book each month. Take down the old one first of course. It was beginning to look impressive, this folder of free materials. She couldn't believe her own generosity. Loss leaders, they called them, didn't they?

It was good for sharing material as well wasn't it? For when they were doing joint edits. She gave other people access rights. They were allowed to edit. It was a bit irritating, though, when they undid one of the edits she'd already completed. It was the whole point, though, she told herself. She must stop being so precious.

The box became full. She was spending more and more time deciding what to keep and what to do away with. The site kept telling her to upgrade to business.

Finally she pressed the button. She calculated how much more a month she needed to earn to justify this. In fact, though, it was harder to find the time to work because the business model came with so many fascinating extra features that she had to learn to justify the cost.

37. Handwritten

The day was grey and miserable. That suited her mood though. There could be nothing good about today. Had it all been a mistake? This isolated house and turning her back on the well-paid safe job in the big city.

The post thudded on to the front door mat. Nothing good ever came through the front door. And she avoided the post girl anyway. She couldn't counter that sullen face and abrupt manner.

She supposed she ought to go and pick it up. Oh, yes. Just as she'd thought. Bills, bills and more bills. Brown envelopes. White envelopes. Some of them – most of them in fact – had red writing on them.

That one looked a bit different though. A London post mark. She trembled as she opened it. No. Why had she got so excited? It was just another rejection. Not even a personal one. Just the standard little slip.

She sighed.

Then the doorbell rang. It was the post girl holding out what looked like a card. "I forgot this. It's too big to go through the door. Somebody's birthday or summat?" The girl was frowning. She didn't wait for a reply.

Birthday? No thank you. She didn't want that. It wouldn't be for several months. That would be something else to be miserable about though at least it would be a few years nearer to the time when she could collect the state pension.

She held her breath as she opened the card.

Class 9E. Thank yous. Little verses.
"We miss you."
"Will you come back next year?"
"Thank you. My dad's really proud of my poem."
All beautifully handwritten.
So, perhaps it was worth it after all.

38. Smart Pad

It was beige and beige, bland-to-earth colours. The whole place smelt of paint and new carpet.

He could hear his neighbours chatting. He couldn't make out what they were saying but they reminded him of his loneliness. There had been two of them before Sophie kicked him out three weeks ago.

He switched on the TV. All his favourite channels were there and he could even access Netflix, but no longer the one he used to share with Sophie. And there was nothing he wanted to watch.

He tried surfing the net instead. He didn't know what he was looking for and he certainly wasn't interested in dating sites yet.

Perhaps he should try the gym. In fact, he was determined to make use of this convenient facility. There was a swimming pool and workout room in the basement that came as part of the deal. In fact it wasn't a real basement, just because it was below street level. It had view across the river into town.

There was another man working out there. He was about the same age as Gary. He nodded. "You too mate?"

"On your own you mean?"

"Yep. Most of us are in the same boat here. In a one-bed cell. The ladies get to keep the big house."

Gary pursed his lips. Yes, Sophie was keeping it all and he was having to pay for it.

"It's not so bad. You get used to it. A lot of us meet up in the bar every night at ten. Come join us."

As he entered the bar later and heard the buzz Gary reflected how lucky he was to afford such a smart pad.

39. BJ

Why does he always have to muss his hair like that? Evem before a radio interview? Okay, so they're filming him going into a radio interview. He has to keep up appearances. Actually, would a fine haircut make a difference? Probably not. He's one of those guys whose shirt always hangs out.

They say he tells lies. Lie after lie, some claim. It's not just the twisting of statistics to suit his cause – that's what most of them do – but he doesn't even trade in verifiable facts, does he?

Of course, he's given us a bit of a giggle at times. They've even liked him on the mainland because he lightens things up. Gives them something to laugh at when things have got too serious. The trouble is, things are serious now and there isn't any time for buffoonery.

He rarely gets his facts right and he ought to be able to, given the education he's had. I know he's just being lazy. Can't be bothered to find out and now it's become a trademark so he can't drop the act even if he wanted to.

Good for the country, eh? Well I suppose at least he'll get on with it. He'll charge in there. Rummage around a bit. Fix a few things, break a few things. Perhaps he will bring us together. He'll unite us in our despair of him.

It's all one great big Eton mess, with a little Jack Russell jumping up at their heels as the cream, meringue and strawberries go flying. Oh oh.

Tweedledee and Tweedledum either side of the Atlantic. But which one is Dee and which one is Dum? Or dumb and dumber?

40. Last Day of the Academic Year

They're off to school for the last time this academic year and it's warm enough for them to be in T-shirts and shorts. They giggle. There's going to be an "it's-a-knockout" challenge. Then they'll be shown their classrooms for next year. How nice. Then they'll sort out things to bring home from the tired display.

But my freedom's gone now. I'll miss the sweet lull after the storm, being able to sit with a coffee and the newspapers, getting the housework done quickly and then spending hours at my desk until it's time for them to come home.

How am I going to keep them busy and happy all day every day? Shall we do nature walks? Collect things? Do little projects? Can I take them swimming? We'll go for a few days to Granny and Grandpa for sure. There will be the bluebell woods at the bottom of the garden and Granny will surely do some baking with them. We'll raid the local library. On rainy days we can make things. Maybe we'll go to the cinema a couple of times.

It'll cost a little, though won't it? And then we'll also have to get ready for the new school year. They grow so much and I guess they'll shoot up even more over the summer.

It's time to go. They mustn't be late, even on the last day of term. They skip along, greeting their friends as we meet them along the way. Even the teachers look cheerful. Well, they'll have a rest tomorrow and the sun is lovely today.

I catch their excitement. Six whole weeks now away from the desk and spending time with my children.

41. A Black and White Maus

The cover fascinates me. Maus. Like mouse. Two anthropomorphic mice stare out. They huddle beneath a stylised cat and blood-red swastika. They are three-dimensional and coloured. I gently touch the cover. My hand trembles slightly. Art Spiegelman. An apt name. A mirror to the world through art.

The swastika threatens. Has that symbol always done that? Was it innocent once? I tentatively touch the cover. It does not hurt me. It is after all just paper, though I continue to shudder.

Yet I am compelled to look more closely. I take it from the shelf and leaf through its pages. It claims to be a survivor's tale. "My father bleeds history and here my troubles began," says Spiegelman. The pictures inside are black and white. It follows true comic bock traditions: read picture and text top left corner to bottom right, lower case for "stage directions" and uppercase for speech, and textures created by arranging lines differently.

I recognise the story too. I've read it before. I've even written it: World War II, concentration camps, survival.

I cannot resist. I move towards the till. I hand the book to the sales assistant and take out my card wallet. She confirms that I get a discount as I am a member of the Society of Authors. "A classic, isn't it?" she says. "Nicely done."

Why have I taken this book? It can't be a comfortable read. I know though I'll admire the artistry, the story-telling and the feel of the book in my hands.

As I make my way to the tram stop I think of that Holocaust: the blame, the hatred, the injustice and hope that it isn't coming back.

42. Their Path

"Now then, guys, smile." A faint breeze came off the Ship Canal. It was good to be near water on a day like this. The photographer danced around them. "Good, good."

Gary and Barry felt good as well. It hadn't always been like this, though. Gary twanged the waistband on his jogging pants. "Remember how we couldn't get anything to fit."

Barry nodded. He remembered uncomfortable clothing that dug into him everywhere. And the sweat. Oh the sweat. Buckets full. A day like this would have probably killed him.

The embarrassment was the worst though. When you took up too much room on the tram, when you began to stink even though you'd used deodorant or when you couldn't bend over to tie up a shoe lace that had come undone.

Then it had become frightening when you got out of breath just walking from the bedroom to the kitchen. When it hurt your lungs just to breathe. And when they told you that they couldn't do the operation on your knee because the anaesthetic would be too risky so you just had to put up with the pain.

Worst of all was not being able to do things with the kids. He couldn't stand through a football practice. He couldn't drive his daughter to ballet lessons because he couldn't fit in the car. Holidays were out of the question.

He and Gary had decided they must do something. Slimming clubs were no good. They couldn't get there. So it had to be online.

It had worked. Who'd have thought it? And now they were advertising it to others.

"Just one more," said the photographer. "Now, smile for the camera."

43. New Book

Gaynor opened the package as quickly as she could. Why did they always have to make them so difficult to open? Then at last there it was. She'd seen the cover before but it looked better in the flesh. What a clever design.

She opened it randomly. She recognised the words. They were hers. Yet they seemed to have been written by someone else now that they were single-spaced and a 8" by 5" book. It even smelt good.

The launch would be in ten days' time. The local bookshop had ordered fifty copies. Her sister Suzy was baking a cake to look like the book. She was supplying some wine and other nibbles. She had a brand new frock and she'd invited over 200 people. They'd never all get in. Someone would come, though, surely?

She sniffed the book once more and then put it down. Now she had to work on social media. She knew she mustn't say "Buy my book, buy my book". She'd got to think of all of those ways of enticing people to read without explicitly saying that they must buy the book. She had a few guest blog posts to do. That might start the ball rolling.

What if she got bad reviews, though? Or no reviews? Which were worse, bad reviews or no reviews, or even perhaps the thought that people were only posting good ones because they were her friend?

Why had she done this?

Her phone rang. Sally. Gaynor's tummy flipped. She knew Sally had started reading the book the day before. The Kindle version had come out earlier.

She accepted the call.

"Fabulous," said Sally. "Absolutely yummy. Well done."

44. Vote Leave

What is this, BJ, a *red* tie? And for once the hair is relatively flat, neat almost. Did you forget to muss it? You look serious for once. Why is that? Will you get your facts right this time? Will you stop joking about not understanding?

"Never have so many…?" Ah. You're trying to be clever. Unfortunately the article is paywalled so we can't read the rest of it. You're saying, though, that these people made a huge decision that's going to make a huge difference? It was actually a *minority* of even the people eligible to vote let alone of all the people who pay their taxes here.

And the lies. Oh the lies. The £350,000,000 a week bus lie. So the farmers now can produce whatever they feel like producing but who will they sell it to? And what will they do if they can't sell these new products? Who will make up for their lost subsidy? Ah, I know. The tax-payer… except aren't; you cutting taxes for those most able to pay them?

What will we do without that lovely EU money that helped us build our roads and improve our public transport? That helped our arts organisations? Because pay those people and you help the world go around. What compensation are a few scrawny food-mile-rich Japanese chickens?

You're supposed to be an intelligent guy. More intelligent than that expat who voted Leave and now regrets it because hey-ho over three years on he's realised that his freedom of movement had been curtailed, and in particular his little dog will lose his pet passport. So come on. Be honest for once.

It just won't work. Please, BJ.

45. Beast of a Car

This was the car he'd always wanted. He touched the metallic blue paintwork. A thrill, a mini orgasm, ran thought his arm and up to his shoulder. Those wheels could tackle any terrain, surely? He felt dizzy with excitement as he smelt the new leather of her seats.

"Go on. Take the twenty-four hour test drive. You know you want to."

He nodded at the dealer and climbed into her. He pressed the ignition button and he was away. Smaller cars and big lorries got out of his way.

Soon he was out of the town, cruising through farmland and the out on the moors. Everyday life was left behind.

The road became rougher and rougher. It didn't matters. She held her own.

She was made for going off road. He turned the steering wheel sharply to one side and they left the road. It felt different under the wheels now but still she kept on going,. She was made for this.

There were no lights or buildings now. It was getting darker and darker. He had plenty of fuel and the vehicle almost seemed to be finding her own way between obstacles. Hadn't the salesman said she could almost drive herself?

He had the sudden curious thought that he might not ever return. He shivered.

The mountains were right in front of him now. Still he drove on. The nearest one seemed to open, as if there were a door there. He accelerated and drove on right into it. The light inside was blinding. He pushed his foot urgently on the brake and hoped the car would stop before they hit anything.

He now knew he would never return.

46. Breaking-up

Enough was enough. What should he tell her? How should he tell her? How would she react? The freedom would be welcome. He could be himself again. Watch the football if he wanted to. Go to the pub to meet his mates. No more Sundays with her parents.

She made a joke of it. Scally instead of Scully. How would she feel if he called her Scally instead of Sally?

Then there were the dishes always left festering in the sink but never washed. Even though they had a dishwasher.

"You always complain when I load it up," she said. "You always rearrange it. You take more time sorting it out that it used to take to wash up. There's no point."

She was always at him to cut the grass as well.

"You're stronger than me. You've got the muscles. I haven't. Go on."

And she wanted him to keep the bushes trim. And dig out the weeds. While she did the fun stuff: putting in new plants, harvesting the fruits and pruning back the perennials.

How to do it, though? Just pack his bags and leave? Take her out for one last meal at Abby's? Send a text?

Well, he was going to pack anyway.

His phone rang.

It was her.

"Hello?" he said. His mouth was dry.

"Listen, I'm on my way to the airport. With Scally. We're going to Tenerife. I'm not coming back. If you could go away, please, the weekend after next I'll move my stuff out. I don't want to see you again. Better this way. A clean break. I'm sorry. I've fallen for Scally."

He started to laugh and then couldn't stop.

47. Fix You

M-Sarah dropped the plate which smashed into the tiled floor. The humanoid bit her lip. "Why do I pay all this money for a machine that can break the crockery even more spectacularly than I can? Where's the sense?"

M-Sarah started the diagnostics straight away. "I will find the problem," she said. "It will be fixed within an hour and the plate will be reprinted."

"You'd better. Or it's back to the factory for you."

M-Sarah ran a full physical test. There was nothing to report. All joints and levers were working perfectly.

It must be to do with the data centre. She initiated a data scan. All software appeared to be working. No bugs. No glitches. No crashes.

So could it be a connectivity problem? A lack of communication? She now ran a series of tests that made sure every physical part responded effectively to the messages from the data-centre. All was working perfectly.

There was nothing to fix. This state of the art self-fixing robot was functioning exactly as it should.

"Well?" The humanoid was frowning.

"It seems to have been an error of judgement."

"Is that even possible?"

M-Sarah shrugged. "We're only ever as good as the people who programmed us."

"But you're supposed to be immune to human error."

"Apparently not. Do you suppose I'm becoming human?"

"Ye gods. I hope not."

A clunk and whirr from the printer now confirmed that the plate had been manufactured. At least she could still multi-task. She'd copied one of the other plates and monitored the printer while she was completing the other checks. In future she would just have to concentrate more when she was unloading the dishwasher.

48. First in Line

He took off his glasses and wiped his forehead. His eyes looked tired. He put his spectacles back on and started to talk. He didn't get eye contact with us. He just looked down towards the left. He didn't seem to be looking at the papers in front of him.

Then he stared right out to us. "You are the first in line."

He cleared his throat. "There will of course be some conditions. You will have to lift your ban on certain substances. You will use more pesticides on your farms and you must wash your meat in chlorine.

"Your health system must be overhauled. It is failing. We recommend that you start using private insurance companies as we do. You must curb your infant mortality rate and you must do better on cancer survival.

"We want you to consider reintroducing the death penalty. Don't you think it will be a real deterrent to those who think it is fine to commit crimes against humanity?

"Yes there will be some demanding changes. But you have your sovereignty back now. No more kowtowing to a foreign power. No more having to accept millions of health tourists and other immigrants. You will make your own laws and you won't be restricted by those living closest to you.

"Yes, my friends, you have your freedom back. You are free to engage with the whole world. You can please yourself what you do about climate change – if there is any such thing. No need to meet those exacting standards any more.

"Welcome to the free world, my friends."

People got to their feet and applauded. Jason and I started a slow hand clap.

49. Hunger

What to do? Tom's money wouldn't come until next week. Geraldine needed to top up the electricity or she wouldn't be able to cook tonight and it was important to keep the kids warm wasn't it? Her part-time job was supposed to stop this but Jamie had needed new shoes. There was one thing she could do, she knew. She didn't like it but it would have to do this time.

She'd always donated herself, hadn't she, when times had been better. It's just that it felt like giving up.

"What are we having for tea?" Allie was nearly always hungry. Geraldine knew she wasn't getting enough. She couldn't let the children get ill. Or they'd take them away from her.

"I'm not sure. We've got to go out first."

It took a while to get there – it always was a rigmarole getting them dressed for outdoors. It was a long walk too but she couldn't afford the bus fare to get them into town.

"Just choose what you want," said the woman who reminded her a bit of her own mother. "Maybe pasta and a sauce? And take a couple of tins to tide you over. And some treats."

"Thank you."

"Thank you." echoed Jamie.

"I know what," said the woman," I'm not really supposed to do this but would you like these?" She held out two shiny red apples. "I'd never manage them all and they only came in big packs of four."

Later after the children were fed and put to bed Geraldine watched the early evening news. "Despite the effects of Brexit," said the presenter, "England remains one of the wealthiest nations in the world."

Really?

50. Blue

A girl with a tear flowing down her cheek looked at her from the mirror. A badly bruised girl. On auto-pilot she applied foundation and blusher to her cheeks and curled her lashes with her mascara. She was presentable again.

Who was this girl? Was she the one who had fallen in love with Tony? She closed her eyes as she remembered being in his arms. He'd held her tenderly and she'd thought he'd loved her too.

But no. It had all been about sex. He'd pushed her and pushed her until she'd given in. It had been more like rape, really, only she couldn't prove that. It had hurt. And then he'd lost interest in her and started seeing another girl.

The little white powder had been such a comfort. There was first of all the thrill of getting it. The risk, then success, and finally the euphoria. But it was too expensive and it was getting too dangerous. She'd got to come off it now. And that was miserable.

She opened her eyes again. The young woman staring back at her looked all right. She knew otherwise though. Here was a complete loser. Somebody who would just not get anywhere. Someone who hadn't got the guts to live life to the full without some chemical help.

The door to the bathroom was suddenly flung open. "We did it Jess." It was her bestie, Pam.

"We did? Which scenes?"

"All of them."

Wow. Perhaps she wasn't so bad after all. It would look really good on her CV. Even if she was only an extra this time, it was for one of the most prestigious soaps for young people.

51. Ego Trip

This photo was going to look good. Really super. Big Ben was in the background. A gentle breeze ruffled her shoulder-length hair a little. It made her look younger. The pearls, though, confirmed her sophistication. That green was her best colour and the smart but simple navy jacket would make people take her seriously. She gazed towards the camera.

Gosh she'd been at this a long time, hadn't she? Back in her uni days she was the one challenging the outside speakers and arranging the protest marches. What was the matter with young people today? They didn't get involved, did they?

Oh that night when she won her first seat.

"Very well, done ma'am," said the rotund chairman of the local group. What was his name? She'd forgotten. "You are so young. I'm sure you'll do a grand job."

Well she had, hadn't she? And now here she was, still in place. Despite all of the turmoil. She'd retained her place. And now she was looking forward to more debates in the House. They may not stop for a summer recess this year, what with all the problems. Bring it on!

It was a real mess, wasn't it? One buffoon in charge and an incompetent anti-Semitic trying to take his place with a third flexing her muscles and elbowing her way in. What a lark.

She would show them. She would throw her clever phrases around. She would challenge the egocentric Eton Mess throwing male chauvinists and the wimpish simpering apologies for women. It was a matter in the end for who would have the last word, wasn't it? She would show them.

"Smile for the camera," said the photographer.

52. No More Water

The net was empty for the seventh day in a row. Not even any seaweed today.

"Look," said Melissa.

"What?"

"Don't you see? The boats are even lower in the water today."

Yes they were getting lower every day. This last ocean was evaporating.

"The water must be going somewhere," she said.

Frank couldn't reply; his mouth was too dry. He thought of the days when they all carried water bottles. Plastic monstrosities. Dehydration had been a myth. Sure, it was uncomfortable but you didn't die of it.

They arrived home.

"I'll go and look in the garden," said Melissa.

Frank nodded. But he knew she would come back without anything. It was all dying. She surprised him though.

"These might cook up." The cabbage leaves were dry and powdery. They might have worked if there'd been any water to cook them in but he doubted they'd come to much baked in the oven.

A squirrel ran across the fence, followed closely by another. Soon a fight broke out.

"I've never seen them that viscous before," said Melissa.

"They're as desperate as we are." They both watched as the bigger squirrel killed the other.

"What?" Melissa screamed.

Frank shook his head. "He's not eating him. He's just drinking his blood."

Melissa didn't eat her dinner. Frank had little appetite for his. It tasted vile and the incident with the squirrel had been upsetting.

"I'm going to bed," said Melissa.

He joined her half an hour later. That was it. That had to be their final meal. He felt under the bed and found the hypodermic they'd saved for this occasion. "Sleep well my lovely," he said as he injected her.

53. Statistics

"You should take a look at this," Jake called from his study.

Suzy put down the pile of linen she was carrying and went into Jake's room. She tutted. "Still on X? Come on, there's work to be done." She wished he'd get on and plant those shrubs they'd acquired yesterday.

She glanced at his computer screen. Yet another poll. Oh heck, though, that didn't look right. "Can you trust it?"

Jake pointed to a familiar icon in the corner of his screen. "It bona fide, look."

Yes it was. Still only statistics, and everybody knew about them, but even so.

Jake leaned back in his chair. "Well, the man's a fool. Everybody knows that."

Suzy nodded. A fool all right. He could never get his facts right, he mussed his hair before every interview even when he it was to be on radio and he was chumming up with that other ridiculous buffoon on the other side of the Atlantic. She sighed. "What's even more worrying is that some people think he's doing the right thing. They're even more idiotic than him. I think he knows what he's doing even though he pretends to be stupid."

Jake nodded. "Yes, those figures are worrying."

Suzy looked a little more closely at the chart. 34% trusted him totally, 55% didn't trust him at all and 12% didn't know. How could they not know?

At least 55% to 34% was a more respectable majority than the 48% 52% split that had caused all the trouble in the first place.

"A pleasant surprise," said Jake.

"Really? I'm not so sure about the pleasant. But yes, I'm astounded that that many actually trust him."

54. Hallucination

Mike had never been to this part of the woods. He'd never gone this far in. He hadn't realised they spread so far. But he had to keep going, for somewhere in the distance he could hear music. It was getting louder now.

The woods were getting wilder. Pathways were now covered up. His legs, bare from the knee down, were covered in scratches. The trees grew close to each other here. It looked as if they hadn't been managed for centuries.

He found himself in a clearing. There was the piano and its player, surrounded by a sizable audience. They were all stocky figures. The player finished one piece and they clapped. Mike joined in. A man near to him turned to face him – except it wasn't a man – it was a – bear?

Mike's mouth went dry and his heart started to thump. What was this? Bears in evening dress and one of them playing the piano? Mike started backing away.

"We don't usually see your kind in these parts," said the bear. "But you are most sincerely welcome to join us. What do you think of Alberto's playing?"

He must be dreaming, mustn't he? Bears couldn't dress or speak so elegantly, let alone play the piano. Had he eaten something that had upset him? Had he been on the jungle juice again? He couldn't remember taking anything but maybe he had.

"Come, come," said the bear. "You look like a chap who would appreciate fine music."

The pianist started up again and Mike turned and began to run. He didn't stop until he was back at the familiar main road and in sight of the number 136 bus.

55. Pie Charts

"Just look at this." Cindy pointed to her screen. "It's worrying."

Arnie looked at the pie chart. Why green, yellow, blue and orange? Green for go, he supposed. The sections looked reasonably even though yellow was the biggest and yes, green for go was next.

"What does this mean, 'couldn't vote'," he asked.

"All those people who pay taxes here but don't have full citizenship? People whose postal votes were lost? Those who have the right to vote but didn't register in time?"

"Yeah, I guess. And those who didn't vote?"

"Unbelievable, isn't it? I do know that some of my students were confused about where they could vote. I wish they'd get their act together and figure it out. It's no good moaning if they don't like the outcome."

"Darn!" Cindy stamped her foot. "They wouldn't let a Trade Union call a strike on those figures."

Arnie studied the figures: yellow 18,604.470, green 17,410,742, blue 16,141,241, orange 12,949,28. More people living here and not allowed to vote than those who voted for this crucial decision?

"And he calls this an 'instruction'? How is this an 'instruction'? The damn thing was only supposed to be advisory. The clue's in the name. They were referring to the people, not getting an instruction from them."

She started typing furiously.

"You job is to assert and defend what you consider to be the national interest, so get to it you great big plonker. And tell your mates too."

He put his hand on her shoulder. "Clam down love. You're putting your blood pressure up again."

She nodded and sighed. "I expect I'm going to get arrested soon." Then she grinned. "Bring it on."

56. Colours

What to wear? What to wear? Could she say it in colours? A blue jacket. That was a lie. But didn't blue represent lies now? The red rosette said it loud enough, didn't it? She knew her black shirt and black hair set it off well enough. And what of the crucifix? Oh yes, indeed. Red lips pouting to boot. She was arriving.

She would always stand up for the working class. Working class? Those who had to work for their money, who didn't get given it.

Not for her the yellow bellies. Broken promises to the students and this absurd pipe dream of maintaining the status quo. Ye gods. The people had spoken and said what they wanted. 52% of them. (Sort of.) Come on. Get on with it.

She touched her jacket lightly. A pity it was blue. The colour suited her. She could never be blue. Especially with the almighty mess they were making now. The whole caboodle an argument between a couple of public school boys. Shame on them. What were they thinking? Their mothers should talk to them seriously.

"I'd rather get into bed with the Jack Russell. I despise what he stands for with his racism, hatred and division. They'll crucify me for sure. But so be it. The people have spoken; I'm not alone in my party thinking this way."

On cue the young man in the purple beanie jumped up in front of her and cried. "The will of which people? Those who were lied to? Those who pay taxes here but aren't allowed a voice? Those who've changed their minds? Those who were too young to give their opinion back then?"

57. Rabbit in a Pink Cage

Gavin thought he was seeing things. There was a rabbit in a huge pink cage in the middle of the hallway. It was quite a cute bunny, actually, mainly black, with a couple of white patches around its ears and nose. Its cage was oh so very pink. It waggled its nose at Gavin.

"Tell me I'm dreaming, Maddy," he called. "I can see a black and white rabbit in a pink cage."

"You're not dreaming, Gav."

"Why?"

"The kids are looking after him over half term. He's house-trained, they say."

"House-trained?"

"Yes, he can be let out and he goes back into his cage to poo." Maddy was now at the top of the stairs. "Oh, and he doesn't eat the electrical wires like that other one used to."

"When did we agree to this?"

Maddy giggled. "We didn't. I arrived at school and there were Toby and Marie just standing there. Fait accompli I'm afraid."

"How the fuck did you get him here?"

"On the tram of course. How else?"

Gavin looked at the cage again. It was a wooden sturdy thing. It must have weighed a ton.

"And did you bring his food and stuff.

"Er, no. That's why we're going shopping."

"We are?"

Toby and Marie burst out of the lounge. "Daddy, what do you think of Patch? We've got him all week. Can we go and get him some food and some straw?"

"I guess."

Well they needed to go food shopping anyway. How would a bag of rabbit food and rabbit bedding hurt? He just hoped that Patch wouldn't die on them like the class gerbil had. Always the nightmare with the class pet.

58. Cloudscapes

It was a pretty decent day for the 19 September. Too hot for a jacket and no need for a raincoat. There were a few clouds but they were friendly white ones, forming stories as they chased across the sky. It was pleasant lying here, the last day but one of his vacation. Next week the office, today the smell of new-mown grass, the sound of a waterfall tinkling nearby and the wonderful warm sun on his face. The grass was even dry. This felt more like July than September.

Now the cloud formed a bear. It stood on its hind legs and punched the air. It was ferocious and cross. But then it started to change shape. It became a creature on four legs again and it was charging, its nostrils flaring. An angry bull. That cloud had a dark edge. Would it rain after all?

What was he thinking? Bear? Bull? He was on holiday, for goodness sake. Why was he thinking about the stock market on holiday? Of course it never went away and if you took your eyes off it it might attack you from behind. He couldn't look at it just now though. The Wi-Fi in the holiday let didn't work.

A cloud moved to his right so that the branch of a tree looked like a tick. The tree's leaves were still green so the message seemed emphatic. So what was it telling him? That he had got it right? What had he got right?

A breeze tickled his face. Yes that was it; he should truly be on holiday and take advantage of this moment. Next week would come soon enough. No worries.

59. The Sandcastle

"Here comes another one," said Marcus. He patted the bucket. Now they had ten little towers in a circle.

"I'll take a photo," said Janine.

Jodi frowned. "They need flags, Grandma. You know the ones with the blue and red crosses."

"I think he means Union Jacks," said Marcus.

They were in France making the most of the late autumn sunshine and easy travel before Brexit kicked in. She doubted whether any shops would be open. "I'll see what I can do."

Of course there were no signs of any Union flags. "We used to have a few packets of the mixed ones," said the assistant in the one shop still selling beach items. "They always had a few. But these are all we've got now." The girl handed her a packet of European flags.

Those would have to do, Janine supposed. Marcus would be delighted: he was always boasting he was a Boomer Remainer and proud of it. But what would Jodi think?

She seemed to go a different way back and found herself looking at the DD Memorial. "Men will be proud to say I am a European. We hope to see a Europe where men of every country will think as much of being a European as belonging to their native land. We hope that wherever they go on the European continent they will truly feel here I am at home," she read. Churchill.

Hmm. She hoped Jodie would see it that way.

When she got back to them Jodie ran up.

"Sorry they hadn't got the sort you wanted."

"I like these even better," said Jodie.

Marcus nodded. "Better build another eighteen towers then, I reckon."

60. The Man in the Suit

He seems trustworthy, the man in the suit. He is in his early fifties, perhaps. His hair is grey and his eyes look sincere. His skin is wrinkled. He could be a headmaster, a GP or somebody's dad. They can all look the same. I've heard him use some common sense before but now he is being questioned. We've all trusted grey-haired men with clear blue eyes and they've let us down.

Now he's saying free trade everywhere is not such a good thing though others are saying it creates economic growth and helps to end child poverty. We need the growth and child poverty must end, though what we mean by it isn't all that clear.

Twenty-eight countries, closely situated to each other, trade freely at the moment. Our wines and cheeses, our fruit and vegetables, our butter and milk are not taxed and don't travel far. Do you remember when the Mediterranean crop failed for a few weeks and we had to import peppers and tomatoes from other continents? The price trebled. Some of it was tax, yes, but much of it was transport costs. We want that? Really?

And this group of twenty-eight countries has great trade deals with other nations and continents. They're probably better than we can negotiate ourselves.

Can you hear the roar of the jet taking off? Do you know how much damage each flight makes? Can you see the smog hanging over most big towns?

In the capital a man is arrested for arguing that we are about to become extinct. Some men, like the one in the suit, shout vile words at an angry but sincere young woman who demands change.

61. Same Old, Same Old

Graham sighed. Another book. Didn't they say there was only one story? This story would follow one of Christopher Booker's seven basic plots, or he'd meet one of Joseph Campbell's thousand heroes who was following Christopher Vogler's journey. There would be a mid-point and a three act structure. The beats would be in the right places.

The cover was gruesome. There was blood spattered across a windscreen.

He flicked open the first page. So where was this inciting incident? And the growing complexities? When would the crisis point arise and would it be convincing? Would the hero get help from an ugly girl and would he live in the belly of the whale for a while? Would he meet the goddess?

It was a nuisance the way this critical mind of his kept interfering. Why couldn't he just enjoy a book these days? Reading used to be his default activity. Now, though, he felt under pressure to read a hundred books a year and review most of them. Where had the fun gone?

"Time to get the G&Ts ready," Louise called from the kitchenette of their small holiday apartment. It was her turn to cook and that half hour before dinner was sacrosanct.

He sliced the lemon mindfully. He put the slices in the glasses, added some ice cubes, counted to ten twice as he poured out the gin, then topped up the drinks with tonic.

As he sipped his drink, sitting comfortably on the glorious terrace with its expansive sea views, he began to read. He stopped noticing the views and was soon absorbed in the story. The editor in his head shut up. This was indeed well written.

62. Propaganda

Someone had made those words into a poster and put them on Instagram. He would see them all as an enemy and make them so uncomfortable he would make them want to leave? Yes, well, he'd probably said those words but he hadn't yet turned them into propaganda. Was that about to come?

Tom knew of course that the racism and the xenophobia had always been there and had bubbled away under the surface. He remembered the kids he'd taught. "Why should I want to go to Frogland? They stink and they eat snails." The finger under the nose and the raised arm that accompanied "Pickled cabbage? Yuk." Well they wouldn't do that in Lancashire. But even the adult had said without shame: "Mañana, Mañana. They're a lazy lot aren't they?" Oh hadn't he done his best – and often succeeded – to get them out of all of that?

It had stayed there though. Ready to be resurrected.

And here it all was now, out in the open. Did that mean, though, that they could at least deal with it?

He did not get one thing though. The man was married to a German. Why hadn't she left him? Did he have too much money? Was she hanging on, trying to persuade him otherwise?

Then he remembered the work he'd been doing on trying to find out why ordinary decent Germans had become Nazis. The glorious Hitler Youth. Kinder, Küche, Kirche. The beautiful BDM girls. Lebensborn. The master race. Aryan blood. Was that it?

He looked again at the document he'd been studying earlier. Too many people recently had been trying to fiddle with Human Rights. Was the beast rising again?

63. The Right Ditch

What the heck? Someone had even put a photo of him and his name on it. And the word "Reserved", just like you might for a table in a restaurant or a hotel room. It was a nice wide ditch and deep. It was absolutely filled with dirty water.

Suddenly he remembered the cold showers that had been a part of every weekday morning when he was at school. He only realised later that it was just the effect of the older boys, who went in first, and used up all the hot water. When he himself got older showers were hotter.

Well, a mere ditch wouldn't hurt that much would it?

He ran his fingers through his unruly blond hair and bit his lip. How had he got to this point? Oh yeah, that cocky little upstart he'd done battle with more recently. Ah, he'd won that round. That twerp had soon scampered away with his tail between his legs.

Oh, but that woman whom he had followed. She could never give a straight answer to anything. And she simpered and stuttered all the time. It made women look bad. He smiled to himself. That at least put the ladies back in their proper place.

But then there was this this major setback. And he had promised, hadn't he? The thing about the ditch. Darn. Didn't the idiots recognise a good metaphor when they fell into one?

Anyway, ditch the ditch idea. There was something much bigger and better to look forward to. He rubbed his hands together in glee and got back into the car. He would get some of his Polish friends to deal with the ditch.

64. The Birds

They can be tiny or gigantic. They can do this thing that we can't. They can stretch out what passes for arms and fly. Oh why can't we? I pause right now to look out of my widow and I can see tits, finches and pigeons.

So, that chain store produced a jigsaw puzzle of British birds but the problem was half of them weren't British. What does that mean, being British? Birds don't have passports do they? If something changes on the planet they may change where they go. Can we learn something here?

Do you member that film? By the guy who always made guest appearances? They didn't use many real birds, though. They spent thousands of pounds on mechanical ones. That film became even more eerie because it had very little music in it – just natural sounds and some calculated silences. The birds fight against humanity, eh? Well, it probably serves us right.

Was it happening again that day, when all of those big birds were lined up on a roof top and kept swooping down on to the road and pecking away at something delicious? As we walked along the road they flew back up to their perch and stared at us.

"Remind you of a film?" asked a passer-by. Yes.

Did you know that many dinosaurs were feathered? And that birds can be traced back to that time? Did they survive by being small enough to live on little after disaster struck?

I look again out of my window. A small tit pecks away at the bird feeder, spilling a few seeds on the ground below for the pigeons. Can't we live side by side?

65. A Poppy's Not Enough

At least they'd let him keep the thick duvet. A street light was shining straight into the doorway. That would help him to keep warm. Tomorrow he'd go to the Town Hall again. This would have to do for now. He buried himself inside the duvet.

He was too cold and angry to sleep. The police had turfed him and the others out of the disused bank. Even he hadn't hit anybody that hard when he'd been a soldier, not even when they'd been at war. The others had been old like him, too. Why would they hit old people like that? He'd been willing enough to move but he was slower on his feet these days. He'd find the others in the morning.

When Ella had died too suddenly and too young he'd not been able to keep up with the mortgage payments. He hadn't got the patience to fill out all the forms. He'd stayed with his son to start with but then she'd got fed up. "I'm sorry Ernie," his daughter-in-law had said. "We can't have you snapping at the kids like that."

He'd stayed with mates for a while. The same problem.

The old bank had been all right. There was even a shower and a toilet but no hot water of course. There had been plenty of comrades.

He felt warmer. The wind had lost its chill. Suddenly he was surrounded by light. He knew what was happening. And yes, there was Ella. And then she wasn't. It was all dark. Was this it?

138

"Thank you for letting us know," said the policeman as the woman fiddled with her poppy. "We'll take it from here."

66. Act of God?

There were still papers on the desks from yesterday's meeting. The chairs were undamaged. If you tucked your trousers into your wellies you could still get into the office without getting wet. The smell was off-putting though. Had the sewers overflowed? It was most likely a health hazard. Best not to go there.

In this room the arguments had been fierce the day before. There were more than two sides, it seemed, and every single person was convinced they were right. As always.

"Climate change is natural. It has happened all the time. Just look at the history books."

"This planet would be better off without us on it."

"People will go mad if they're not allowed their red meat."

"The oil industry and the car industry have a lot to answer for."

"Electric cars are all very well but we don't yet have the infrastructure to support them."

They'd held the vote about whether to accept the Union's proposals on how to tackle climate change and those against it had won by a narrow margin.

Marco watched the workers beginning the clean-up operation. It involved a huge pump. As areas cleared of water the workers began to rip up the damaged floors.

"Have you ever seen anything like this before?" Marco asked a gentleman who looked about as old as his own father.

"No, never." He sounded bitter. "It's an act of God. Because people won't listen. They're too selfish. They just carry on, not caring about the planet." The man stopped working and looked straight at Marco. "So, what are you going to do about it young man? Well?"

Marco guessed it was time to call another meeting.

67. Office Life

"God, it's dull in here today." Gerald sighed. It was always dull in the export/import office. He had hoped that Brexit might liven it up a bit but that had been postponed yet again. And today was typical Rainy City – absolutely pouring.

Jolene started rummaging in the waste paper bin.

"What are you doing?" asked Flick.

Jolene tapped her nose. "You'll see." Half an hour and three glue sticks later the office was adorned with colourful paper chains.

Gerald had an idea. "I won't be long," he said.

He pulled his old parka on so he wouldn't get wet. Yes he was right. One of the stalls on Albert Square was selling some cute little Christmas trees. If Brexit had happened, this lot wouldn't be here.

"I'll get some of those cheap lights from the pound shop on the way home," said Flick when he got back into the office. "And listen to what I've found on my phone." She put it on speaker and clichéd Christmas music started playing.

"What the heck?" It was Reggie Arnold, the boss.

"Just a bit of Christmas spirit, Mr Arnold," said Jolene.

Reggie puffed himself up and Gerald was sure he was going to say "Bah, humbug."

"We've already finished this month's returns," said Flick. "I'm sure a bit if Christmas spirit will get us ahead with December's work. Then there'll be no problem if we get any snow days."

Reggie sighed. "I suppose you might be right." He took a couple of notes out of his pocket and handed them to Gerald. "Go on then. You'd better get a round of those gingerbread lattes."

Gerald grinned and reached out for his parka.

68. Warfare

So we strut and parade, waving our flags and singing anthems. We all wear the colours of the emblems that belong to us. The pictures mean something. Take for example our own, made of three others brought together but where are the dragons? Ah. "We'll beat you in the football, we'll beat you in the tennis and we'll even run faster."

We're all so good, every one of us. We have our culture and our history. You have your fine wines. They have the sunshine. Others are good at draining the seas, reclaiming the land and moving around by water.

"We're not going to be bossed around by you," they say, the quitters. "We'll do what we want to do and not what you tell us to do. Our ways are better than yours." Never mind that you took on board what we suggested and even came up with some of your own ideas that were at least as good as ours or perhaps even better.

Now the borders are shut. We can't visit, even if we want to. We can't emigrate for work. Even if we were allowed to in the future now we can't. Is this a taste of what it's could be like in the worst case scenario? I watch films of places in the sun and long for that glorious opportunity. It's raining here.

Can't we work together to stop this pestilence? Can't we exchange ideas? Can we learn from each other?

There are new ways now. Are we learning something? Do we have some of what you want and can we have some of your abundance? The bird that crosses the mountains pays no taxes.

69. The Marketing Writer

The writer stared at her blank screen. Heavens above! Why must she do this? She was a writer not a marketer, not a car salesman. Couldn't someone else do this? She should be writing.

"Remember the thousands of dollars," a more experienced writing friend had told her. "That is your ticket to giving up the day job soon. That will give you permission to spend your time writing."

She found a picture of bundles of bank notes and pasted it into the document she was working on.

Keep it simple, she persuaded herself. Tell them what they need to know: the title of the book, ISBN, number of pages, release date, what it's about (but a blurb, not a synopsis?), what she was willing to do, when she would be available for interview. Maybe a line or two about why she had the expertise to write this book?

She looked at her handiwork. Yes, it all fitted neatly on to one page of A4. This looked professional. Everything was very clear. What further questions could they ask?

Yes, it all looked competent enough. But it lacked sparkle. Did that actually belong more in the covering email she should send with this perfect press release? Maybe. What should she say?

It came to her suddenly. She should say how this had really been her mother-in-law's story. How she had actually written it for her. How she'd had this wonderful primary resource in a bunch of young women's letters.

That was it. She went through her list, pasted her copy into the body of the emails and attached the press release.

She sat back and waited.

Ten minutes later the phone rang.

70. Get Online 2020

The way around it of course was Zoom. If you couldn't meet in person why not use Zoom? Why not Skype, or Teams, or Web X, though? Because Zoom had more of a ring about it.

Some sat there with pads over their ears, and some had little buds in them. Some had a microphone on their desk. Even sometimes an old-fashioned round one. Like the guy on the telly last night. On the BBC of all things. Who'd have thought it?

He should really get himself set up like that. How much did it cost, that sort of equipment? He searched through his favourite on-line shops. He read the reports. This was the best. And cost-effective. He'd saved more than that by not going to the pub, by not taking the tube and by learning to cook.

So, he filled out the order carefully and tracked it anxiously. It had left the depot. It had arrived in the nearest town. It was less than a kilometre away. There was a van in the street. The doorbell rang.

"It's on the step, mate," the delivery man shouted to him.

He opened the parcel, washed his hands, disposed of the packaging, washed his hands again and set it all up according to the instructions. And washed his hands again.

He opened Zoom and saw himself on the screen. Yes this was it. Now he looked right.

He started letting his people into the meeting room.

"The first news," said Thackeray, the chairman, "is that we have made the office safe. You can all come in again as from tomorrow. This will be the last meeting we need to hold like this."

Like to Read More Work Like This?

Then sign up to our mailing list and download our free collection of short stories, *Magnetism*. Sign up now to receive this free e-book and also to find out about all of our new publications and offers.

Sign up here:
http://eepurl.com/gbpdVz

Please Leave a Review

Reviews are so important to writers. Please take the time to review this book. A couple of lines is fine.

Reviews help the book to become more visible to buyers. Retailers will promote books with multiple reviews.

This in turn helps us to sell more books... And then we can afford to publish more books like this one.

Leaving a review is very easy.

Go to https://amzn.to/47dk6ys, scroll down the left-hand side of the Amazon page and click on the "Write a customer review" button.

Other Publications by Bridge House Imprints

140 x 140
by Gill James

This anthology of women's fiction, this collection of very short stories, some might say a flash collection, is thought-provoking and each story is based upon a tweet. Except that each piece is 140 words long and not 140 characters.

"In this entertaining book, Gill James chose the first picture she saw on her Twitter feed on specific dates. As the title suggests, there are 140 stories, each of 140 words. Some tales are laugh out loud funny, others thoughtful, and there are tragic stories too. Whatever your mood, you will find plenty to suit you here." *(Amazon)*

Order from Amazon:
ISBN: 978-1-910542-35-4 (paperback)
978-1-910542-36-1 (ebook)

Chapeltown Books

January Stones
by Gill James

These stories were written one a day throughout January 2013. They were originally published on a blog called Gill's January Stones. Sometimes the stories would come right at the beginning of the day. Sometimes they would take a while longer.

Do they have a theme? Not really, though the idea of 'stones' is one of turning them over slowly on the beach until we find the right one.

There was no strict word count. Each story is as long as it needs to be. It had to be finished, though, by midnight of that day.

Order from Amazon:

ISBN: 978-1-910542-10-1 (paperback)
978-1-910542-11-8 (ebook)

Chapeltown Books

Other Ways of Being
by Gill James

Other Ways of Being is a an anthology of stories that point us to other times, other histories, other worlds including those of our near futures, other sexualities and other genders.

Order from Amazon:

Paperback: ISBN 978-1-907335-67-9
eBook: ISBN 978-1-907335-68-6

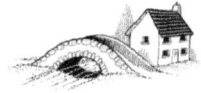

From the Beginning to the End
by Henry Lewi

Sure, there are beginnings and ends and there is all the stuff that happens in the middle.

Begin with the Big Bang and end with a distant trumpet call; understand how to send a cheese sandwich into the future, have the origin of the universe explained, and find out how to achieve immortality; and finally add in a splash of espionage. Enjoy the mix.

"These stories reveal that Henry Lewi has a terrific imagination and a great sense of fun." *(Amazon)*

Order from Amazon:

ISBN: 978-1-915762-15-3 (paperback)
978-1-915762-16-0 (ebook)

Chapeltown Books

The City of Stories
by Lynn Clement

What goes on behind closed doors? Donna and Jim struggle with an unspeakable act. Millicent encounters something that will change her forever, and Marie dreams of being free from her harrowing life. Melvin's pelvic thrusts have his clients in a sweat, and Sister Francis, the bike-riding nun, has her secret revealed.

The City of Stories is a collection of short, easy-read stories and poems that range from dark tales with a twist, to funny flash fiction that will make you laugh out loud.

"An art gallery full of vivid word pictures." *(Amazon)*

Order from Amazon:

ISBN: 978-1-910542-81-1 (paperback)
978-1-910542-82-8 (ebook)

Chapeltown Books